Gleeson White

Christmas Cards and Their Chief Designers

Gleeson White

Christmas Cards and Their Chief Designers

ISBN/EAN: 9783337262624

Printed in Europe, USA, Canada, Australia, Japan

Cover: Foto ©Andreas Hilbeck / pixelio.de

More available books at **www.hansebooks.com**

FROM AN ETCHING BY
EDWARD SLOCOMBE, R.P.E.

CHRISTMAS CARDS AND THEIR CHIEF DESIGNERS BY GLEESON WHITE

LONDON OFFICES OF THE STUDIO
NEW YORK FREDERICK A. STOKES
COMPANY MDCCCXCV

ARTISTS

WHOSE DESIGNS ARE ILLUSTRATED HEREIN

C. J. Horsley, R.A.
H. Stacy Marks, R.A.
W. F. Yeames, R.A.
R. W. Macbeth, A.R.A.
W. L. Wyllie, A.R.A.

R. J. Abraham.
Wilfrid Ball, R.P.E.
W. T. Baxter.
C. H. Bennett.
Randolph Caldicott.
W. S. Coleman.
Thomas Crane.
Walter Crane.
J. M. Dealy.
Herbert Dicksee, R.P.E.
— Dillon.
R. Dudley.
Alfred East, R.I.
Rosina Emmett.
G. Cave France.
C. M. Gere.
Kate Greenaway.
A. H. Haig, R.P.E.
G. C. Haité, R.B.A.
Alice Havers.
Sidney Heath.
Fred Hines.
L. B. Humphreys.
F. G. Jackson.
E. K. Johnson.
Walter Langley, R.I.
E. Blair Leighton.
A. C. V. Lilly.
W. H. Low.
A. Ludovici, Junr.
Fred Mason.
F. S. Mather.
W. Midgley.
W. J. Muckley.
H. F. New.
F. Markham Skipworth.
Edward Slocombe, R.P.E.
H. R. Steer.
S. Thompson.
E. G. Thomson.
Elihu Vedder.
W. J. Wainwright, A.R.W.S.
Alfred Ward.
C. J. Watson, R.P.E.
C. E. Weldon.
Dora Wheeler.
Alice B. Woodward.

CHRISTMAS CARDS AND THEIR CHIEF DESIGNERS

THE fact that the Christmas card is rapidly becoming a recognised subject for collectors would not in itself warrant its consideration from a purely artistic standpoint. For collecting is only accidentally concerned with Art. Some most popular manufactured products, eagerly amassed by experts, could not for an instant be considered even mildly artistic. A postage stamp, for example, that is not absolutely beneath contempt so far as its design is concerned, is rare enough. Comparatively few "book-plates" are in themselves intrinsically interesting as decoration. But other branches familiar to connoisseurs coins, gems, terra cottas, lacquer, bronzes, and the like, are almost invariably artistic, often enough genuinely serious works of art. The Christmas card must be taken as mid-way between the extremes. Perhaps in no single instance does it rise to the level of the average of the best coins, gems, or terra cottas. But even at its worst it is seldom so distinctly unlovely as the postage stamp, or the old play-bill. Such interest as it possesses, however, is entirely confined to its designs. Its sentiment excellent in itself is worn threadbare by repetition. Its "original poetry" is rarely original, still more rarely poetry; its ideals are, as a rule, peculiarly conventional.

For the preparation of this paper, it has been my lot to look through the sample books of all the chief firms who manufacture Christmas cards. How many thousand patterns have passed under my eye I dare not estimate. A complete set of all designs published in England alone would include at least 500,000 examples, possibly

THE FIRST CHRISTMAS CARD (1846) DESIGNED BY J. C. HORSLEY, R.A., FOR SIR HENRY COLE

a good many more, yet of these the number that could be grouped under the various seasonable subjects I have roughly jotted down might be reckoned in hundreds at the most. Flowers, fairies, everything and anything all over the world, in all seasons of the year, have been pressed into the service of the Christmas card. The legends, painfully monotonous in their greeting, are, as a rule, purchaser, is more likely to be ridiculous than apt. Consequently the wisdom of the publishers has generally preserved them from ridiculous excesses of sentiment—so far as regards the message the cards are supposed to bear. "A Merry Christmas," more usually modified to "A Happy Christmas," frequently (I regret to say) abbreviated unnecessarily to "A Happy Xmas," with or without the "to you," may be taken as the representative phrase in ninety-nine out of a hundred instances.

C. H. BENNETT (1864-6)

C. G. AND S.

It is obvious that for the sake of their literature no collection would be worth making. We are, therefore, compelled to own that it is in the design alone that any reasonable excuse can be found; otherwise as objects of sentiment, literature, or documents of social interest, the post-mark or the railway ticket might be collected with not less inconsequence, and with almost as much reason to be reckoned an outlying colony of the empire of art and letters.

The designs, however, have a distinct interest. During the most notable period of production, 1882, one firm alone paid in a single year seven thousand pounds to artists for original drawings. If you turn over the records of sales at the Royal Academy and note the prices, the amount of works "sold" in a season, you will realise that an art patron who spends seven thousand pounds in a year, be he a person or a company, is a very rare creature. What influence this expenditure had upon British Art, either on its own merits, or in comparison with the patronage bestowed upon Burlington House, is too large a subject to enter upon here. It is a fact, however, that for ten or twelve years the cards of many of the prominent makers attracted the work of artists of considerable repute, including not merely several members of the Royal Academy and others already popular, but of men then scarce out of their student days, who have since established themselves as painters and illustrators of the first rank. Yet this period of popularity, when the artist, not accustomed to designing for commercial purposes, was often lured to do so, has fairly well defined limits; from 1878 to 1888, is, roughly speaking, the happy hunting ground

the only common factor it possesses. If it has never descended to the fatuous vulgarity of the valentine, on the other hand, it has rarely risen far above the conventional courtesies of daily life. Its idiom hardly conveys more personal feeling than the commonest colloquial phrases "Good Morning" or "Good-bye." On the whole, this absence of fervour is a thing to be grateful for. A passion poured out in a phrase, to be used haphazard by any chance of the collector. Since that time the designs are for the most part supplied by those who habitually work for colour printers, and one suspects that instead of being almost wholly of British origin, as in those years, a very large proportion of cards to-day are not merely "manufactured in Germany," but designed there also.

The orthodox card attracts you solely by its design. A chromo-lithograph upon a rectangular card, decorative in treatment as a rule, it was content to rest upon the attraction of its subject alone. Now-a-days, from frosted surfaces to fringed edges, from perforated cardboard to pieces of brown paper, old cigar ends, and rubbish of all sorts its catholicity is unbounded. When, however, its limitations were disregarded, its art escaped rapidly.

Hard as it is to define sharply the limits within which artistic interest is to be found, it has been the purpose here to make a rough survey of the ground, to gather together a mass of facts, by no means exhaustive, and to present a cursory summary of the subject, not unlike the tentative pamphlets in favour a century ago modestly entitled: "Contributions towards the History of So-and-so." Starting with the brave enterprise of mastering the subject, collating all the sample books of all the publishers, digesting the facts into formal order, making a complete list of every card worthy of serious note, the result is much more modest than the attempt. For to systematise the chaos of the thousands one had nearly written millions of designs were enough to frighten the most expert catalogue maker. If to this you add the task of deciding where the border line is to be drawn between worthy effort and sheer inanity, it is obvious that even the rapid decision of a Royal Academy jury would be paralysed, that the most learned judge would be appalled by an attempt to summarise the evidence and present a coldly impartial statement of the facts. Indeed, to identify and collect a specimen of each might exhaust a life-time; to classify and appraise them would be like compiling a dictionary. To fail, in the limited time allowed, is to confess one's self human, to succeed would be a task for the genii of the Arabian Nights.

It seems perfectly unnecessary to explain here the object of a Christmas card or, perhaps one might write more truthfully, the object conventionally accepted as the reason for the existence of the custom which has grown up in the last quarter of a century. To find precedents in the "everlasting great Japan" with its almost precise equivalent, the Suri-mono, sent to friends on New Year's Day, would be tempting; but the dignity of our native products might suffer if set side by side with the exquisitely dainty prints familiar to collectors of Japanese art. These, in their employment of metal as well as colour, their embossed surfaces, and the playful grace of their design, may bear somewhat the same relation to the sterner art of the ordinary colour print that our own

C. H. BENNETT (1866-7) C. G. ANDS.

Christmas cards bear to the more ambitious products of the print-seller's window. The difference between an Arundel Society's print and the Raphael Madonna, or one of the Fra Angelico angels, issued as Christmas greetings, is mainly one of size; and the average landscape

H. STACY MARKS, R.A. M. W. AND CO.

of the card is as artistic as the average landscape of the chromo-lithograph or oleograph; but the average figure subject is not so nearly on a par with the ordinary modern picture of the galleries, too seldom reproduced in chromo-lithographs to allow the comparison.

Between the art of the Christmas card and that of the Suri-mono the difference is far more than that between "hand-painted" and printed pictures. In Japan, the Suri-mono is merely the art of the day lightened and treated a little less demurely. In England, even the best of Christmas cards cannot be placed in serious rivalry with a Whistler etching, or a wood-cut of the "Once a Week" school. To us it is rarely given to be "funny without being vulgar," that is to say, when the gaiety is intentional. The true courtesy of Japanese art may unbend and preserve its dignity unimpaired; here, we are apt to grow unduly coarse, as in Rowlandson's caricatures, or Cruickshank's etchings; distinctly bourgeois, as in Hogarth, or the cartoons admirable in their way of *Ally Sloper;* or to be merely "pretty," as in the average colour print.

It is not surprising that the humour of our Christmas card is often even sadder than its sentimental effusions, and they are at times gloomy enough. Indeed, it is amusing to note the pictorial accompaniments considered fit to illustrate the very mundane wish for "A Happy Christmas." As we know, the hope implied is unquestionably that the recipient may be surfeited with turkey and mince pie; have a feast of roast beef and plum pudding, and well-filled stockings if a juvenile; and good entertainment and much jollity if an adult. To accompany this prosaic and wholly carnal greeting we find, often enough, tragic sunsets, haunted churchyards, consumptive choir boys, monsters of nightmareland, pictures of accidents dear to the farce writer, and, in short, the subjects which are in vulgar parlance "weird" and alarming on the one hand, and distinctly uncomfortable on the other. Or to take the opposite extreme: the glory of the transformation scene in a pantomime, the tinselled splendour of stage fairy-land is presented as the haven of our heart's desire. Houris, most scantily attired, are sent to demure stockbrokers; fairies, revelling by moonlight, to grim county magistrates whose sympathy for midnight revels in their preserves would probably urge them to commit the whole

H. STACY MARKS, R.A. M. W. AND CO.

tribe of pixies to the county gaol. So the game is played, or rather was played, for to-day flowers are almost the one idea of the designer. Flowers possible or impossible, mostly the latter, are his chief aim; and, poor as the ideal may be, it is, at least, less unfit than many of the fantastic themes which before figured as the illustration to the conventional recognition of "Goodwill towards Men."

For—and the fact must be only touched lightly here—if we look below the surface, we find these gaudy pasteboards are meant to pass

H. STACY MARKS, R.A. M. W. AND CO.

on from one human being to another the echo of the salutation which sounded in the shepherds' ears that night in far Bethlehem. All this vast industry is to afford a way of expressing one's goodwill to one's neighbours; to send out, not with too personal a meaning, as in a written letter, the assurance of renewed amity; to say as it were, "all through the rest of the year we have not met, and may not do so," or else, "although I have seen you frequently but left this fact unsaid," (it matters not which hypothesis we accept) "yet at this season, when of old a message of peace and friendliness was sent from heaven to earth, I would you should feel I bear you no ill-will, but wish you all good things in the future." This, a settling of outstanding grievances, a balancing of one's social accounts at the end of the year, is the sole defence of the custom worth considering. In such a way new acquaintances, not insufficiently familiar intercourse to exchange letters, may greet each other without presumption. Those to whom one is indebted, those who may, one suspects, feel slighted by omissions in the past, are thus for the moment brought into touch. So for Christmas Day, as the feast is eaten that records the most striking event of the era in which we live, the formal armistice is duly prepared; no matter if we may secretly intend to renew the slight feud in the New Year, it is set aside for the moment, and, in theory, we are at one with the world, and at peace with all men.

To translate this laudable intention into dull facts, to note the ridiculously insincere feeling underlying the custom, would be easy enough: too easy, indeed, for the most cynical person to care to attempt. Everybody is able to search his own memory and discover the very remote resemblance between the idea which governs the sending of a card and the actual reason for its dismissal; but noting that it undoubtedly owes its origin to the birth of the Christ child, it is odd to find in how comparatively few instances it recognises, even remotely, that it is not a secular but a sacred function which is being celebrated.

It would be out of place to dwell upon this tendency to secularise the greetings of the season; but it is impossible to avoid noticing it. For one feels that if the custom had arisen centuries earlier, if Giotto or Botticelli, Raphael or even Overbeek for once "curbed the liberal hand subservient, proudly cramped their spirit, crowded all in little," and essayed a trifle of this sort, then if they had filled their "missal marge with flowerets," it would have been as framework to the subject of the Nativity. The

H. STACY MARKS, R.A. M. W. AND CO.

WALTER CRANE M. W. AND CO.

central fact that the word "Christ-mass" implies would undoubtedly have been taken as the motive of the whole decoration.

It is apparent, also, that if the cards owe little to the symbolism of the past they are equally unconcerned with the portrayal of the present, except so far as feasting and sports are concerned. Politics are, with almost a single exception, absolutely absent. No pictured record of the year whose end they mark is to be found in any of them, no prophetic vision of the sort dear to lovers of Zadkiel's Almanac has intruded itself. Ibsenism, the New Woman, even Aubrey Beardsley, are beyond the ken of their designers. For the current topics of the day they care but little; a mildly satirical anecdote distinguishes a few; but pastimes, even the most inappropriate, are in shoals. Swimming, boating, cricket, tennis, are obviously introduced by way of being personally appropriate to the taste of the recipient, with no regard for its untimely appearance. Mediaeval pleasantries abound on early cards, but the slightest knowledge of the period that welcomed their introduction will readily explain the presence of the Gothic element which was at that time accepted as the English ideal of decorative art. To-day the Rococo is supreme in the furniture shops, and the cards have nearly all adopted its erratic curves and tortured forms; in some cases with really delicate appreciation of the beauty that can be attained in the most abandoned of all styles. The so-called æsthetic period also left its mark; acres of flattened sunflowers and angular damosels were produced when the peacock feather was the oriflamme of cultured folk. To this period also we owe the singularly felicitous decoration of the backs and borders of the cards which Mr Thomas Crane designed so excellently well. In the colour of these, the simplicity of their flat ornament and the artistic fitness, I, for one, find the high water-mark of the card. Not in its reproductions of pictures which are at best imitations (they cannot hope to equal, much less surpass, the original, even should that chance to be worthy, which could not be affirmed of the majority of cards); not in the faultless nicety of register, the brilliant colours, the exquisite gilding and embossing of a later period, nor in the clever studies of flowers, is the ideal of the card so nearly achieved, it seems to me, as in certain simple treatments, obviously printed and aiming to be decorated pasteboard—no less and no more—which Mr Thomas Crane treated so effectively. In saying this it is with no wish to decry the genuine beauty of a hundred other styles, judged from different standpoints, but to insist that for legitimate use of the mere materials, cardboard and printer's ink, for the easy method of securing true decoration by the

WALTER CRANE M. W. AND CO.

WALTER CRANE M. W. AND CO.

most direct means, it would be hard to find in European colour printing anything that fulfilled its purpose more completely. Here, and here only, one feels, has the limit been recognised the question of economic production faced and conquered, and a simple bit of lithography made admirable art, not because of its superb drawing or refined colour, but because of its simplicity, dignity, and absence of imitation.

How many factors were at work to produce the sentiment which accepted eagerly the tentative efforts of the first attempts of the manufacturers is not easy to estimate. The Prince Consort is credited with the introduction of the Christmas tree to English houses, and to Charles Dickens much of the sentimentality, as well as the genuine feeling of the season, is undoubtedly due. Yet the institution of a new custom, which by leaps and bounds grew well nigh universal, must be explained by more than these influences.

So that without an attempt to prove that the introduction of the Christmas card is evidence of democracy, of the world-spirit, or the "new" anything, one must accept a chance experiment of tradesmen (who may or may not have known of Sir Henry Cole's card of twenty years before), as so apt in the moment of its trial, that it induced the most conservative nation in the world to recognise a new courtesy, to institute a new custom, and this not merely in an aristocratic or a democratic way, but unanimously, without question of sect or party, station or social etiquette. From the duchess to the dairy-maid a demand for cards arose. Sent at first to familiar friends only, they gradually became formal tokens despatched to almost every one on my lady's visiting list, or the most distant cousins and acquaintances of those who do not manage their social amenities with the book-keeping absolutely essential for folk in society.

The origin of the Christmas card is, fortunately for its future historians, not lost in the mists of antiquity, that popular hiding place for all sorts of origins; but as clearly fixed as Archbishop Usher's date of Creation (B.C. 4004, October 26, 4.30 p.m.), with more trustworthy evidence to support it. In 1846, Sir Henry Cole (then plain Mr) suggested the idea of a specially designed form of greeting to send to friends at Christmas. Mr J. C. Horsley, R.A., acting on the hint, produced a design of a trellis of rustic-work, in the Germanesque style, divided into a centre and two side panels. In the panels are figures representing two of the acts of charity, "feeding the hungry" and "clothing the naked;" in the centre is a picture of a merry family party, including three generations, grandparents to grandchildren, quaffing draughts of wine. It was

WALTER CRANE M. W. AND CO.

KATE GREENAWAY M. W. AND CO.

lithographed and printed by Jobbins, of Warwick Court, Holborn, and coloured by hand. Only 1,000 copies were issued; they were published under Sir Henry Cole's *nom de guerre* "Felix Summerly" by his friend Joseph Cundall, of New Bond Street. Messrs De La Rue reproduced it by chromo-lithography in 1881.

Despite a suggestion that the idea might have been taken from certain illuminated cards the Germans were in the habit of sending to their relatives, some forty or fifty years ago, on their "*Namenstag*" that is, the feast of their patron saint, not the recipient's own birthday we may claim an English source for the custom now so universal. To find it came, like many other good things, from the direct instigation of one of the best-abused men of the century, so far as things artistic are concerned, will be a joy to its enemies, and a pleasant anecdote for those who feel that the system labelled South Kensington, may, when distance enables a critic to have larger views, prove to have done much practical good in the way it was intended to work, despite all the shortcomings and imperfections, which every art-student has at his finger ends.

To discover that many over-zealous partisans of our temperance cause objected strongly to this design, bridges over the gap of close upon half-a-century, and imparts the flavour of modernity to the half-forgotten incident. What has been started in England that "yearnest" people have not attacked? If we investigated all the cases of drunkenness in all these years, could we find a single one remotely traceable to this design of Mr Horsley's, or any of its fellows?

Thus we see, as in so many other inventions, the steam engine for example, one person originates the idea, works it in a humble way, and, years after, another turns the toy to a machine that re-organizes society. The card Sir Henry Cole started, and the cards that John Leighton designed, are much nearer akin than the steam engine of the Greek (or was it the Egyptian?) to that of James Watt; and yet the analogy is not entirely absent, for, from the time of Watt or of "Luke Limner," the use of steam or of cards ceased not, but increased year by year. To-day, when a certain minority affects to regard the fashion as dying, if not already obsolete, far larger numbers are produced than in its most palmy days. The habit of collecting examples of the best of all years, of completing sets of the designs, and of forming collections of these ephemeral things, is already well on its way to a recognised position among

WE COME THE PRETTY SPEECH TO SAY
WE LEARNED IT FOR YOU ON CHRISTMAS DAY

KATE GREENAWAY M. W. AND CO.

KATE GREENAWAY M. W. AND CO.

hobbies, such as "book-plates" has achieved and "posters" are beginning to obtain. It is to be regretted that the British Museum, omnivorous as it is, has, so far as its catalogue indicates, merely a few dozen specimens. Rumour has it that a collection, if not absolutely comprehensive, yet, for all practical purposes complete, might be acquired at the present time. Despite the apparent insignificance of the subject, so interesting a record of social custom and the development of a large and highly artistic industry of purely English origin, should not be allowed to escape the custodians of our National Museum. If space can be found for complete sets of Railway Time Tables and other records of similar intrinsic value, it would be regrettable did a collection of Christmas cards fail to obtain a place, either there, or at the more appropriate habitation, the home of the Applied Arts, the South Kensington Museum. For if the present generation find them merely "old-fashioned," in a few decades they would appear "quaint" and "curious," and finally be appreciated as very interesting *ephemeræ* of a very interesting period in English Art-production.

Here it would be out of place, even did space permit, to record in detail the productions of each of the various firms in whose hands the Christmas card was shaped to popularity. Yet remembering that the thousands of designs produced in the last thirty years were chosen by a comparatively few manufacturers, one sees that perhaps not more than a dozen men were directly responsible for the artistic course of its rise and decline. For in all the applied arts there is a critical moment that affects them vitally—the moment when the criticism of the maker condemns, approves, or modifies the intention of the artist. It were easy to say that his influence is always for evil; indeed, the temptation to explain the barrier to our artistic progress by heaping all the blame on one class only, is nearly irresistible; because in the case of a very large proportion of those implicated it is a true finding. Yet it would be unfair to ignore the instances to the contrary, and still more unjust to overlook the patent fact that the manufacturer is not himself a free agent. Theoretically he has only his own pocket to consider, but that is a somewhat weighty argument in favour of safe un-experimental work. Setting aside the fact that few large businesses are the property of one person, and that the "Art" partner has to respect the criticisms of his commercial colleagues, he has also to face the prejudice and vulgar taste of a very important factor in the whole matter—the buyer for the trade. This personage, unlike an editor—the middleman for black and white art—usually meets his customers face to face and exchanges direct opinions with them. The ordinary buyer, drawn as a rule from the lower bourgeois class, has absolute ignorance of the traditions of art, but a very decided belief in his own ill-formed taste. He is ready enough to tell you, in unasked confidence, "that he knows nothing about art, but he knows what will sell." Fancy yourself a manufacturer bent on improving your wares, be they carpets or cards, whose every effort to attain a higher standard in design is snubbed by the men whom you employ to sell them to the retail tradesmen, and you will criticise his action less sharply! For it is

KATE GREENAWAY M. W. AND CO.

evident that some such individual, whether called buyer or commercial traveller, comes between the manufacturer and the retailer in almost every instance. Not only has this personage to reckon with the taste of shop-keepers, which varies from the best to the worst, with a tendency to the latter, but he has also his own standard to defend. Hence he sells most readily not only those goods the average retail trader is most likely to choose for himself, but a great many others which, since they approve themselves to the vendor, he can recommend with sincerity.

It is strange that this needle's eye, through which so much Applied Art has to pass ere it reaches the public, is not more often recognised as the chief obstacle to its progress. The public should not be held responsible for declining to purchase goods which never came under its eyes; the manufacturer should not be held blameworthy for the poor level of the Art he offers, when, possibly, he has tried and tried in vain to induce his travellers and the trade buyers to support his efforts to produce good designs.

Although 1846 has been so far accepted as the undisputed date of the first card, just before going to press, Mr Jonathan King, the owner of the largest collection, has called my attention to a paragraph in a journal of some standing, where a Mr Thomas Sherrock, of Leith, is said to be the real inventor of the Christmas card, seeing that a year or two before the above date he issued one, with a laughing face, and the motto "A Gude New Year to Ye." Whether this be the card which is elsewhere said to have been engraved on a copper- plate by a workman, Daniel Aikman, in 1840 or 1841 and published with a Scotch motto, I am unable to prove. Should either of these statements be accurate, although one might, without special pleading, claim that a New Year secular greeting is not quite the same as one marking a religious festival, it would be best to give later inventors equal credit, and assume, what would be probably correct, that neither knew of the doings of the others. So, too, the statement that engravers' apprentices of Northumberland or Yorkshire (the stories differ, and one questions if such a class of artists exists in either place in sufficient numbers to found a custom), are in the habit of sending specimens of their own work to friends at Christmas, and have done so for a long period, may or may not be true, but is hardly likely to have been the source whence the card was derived. Equally difficult is it to obtain any details of Messrs Goodall's cards in 1862 (or 1864, authorities vary,) which were probably the first issued to the ordinary trade. Despite a former sentence crediting Messrs Goodall with the honour of being the first publishers of Christmas cards, (always excepting the Sir Henry Cole card of 1846,) and,

KATE GREENAWAY

M. W. AND CO.

KATE GREENAWAY

M. W. AND CO.

notwithstanding the fact that several of their cards, issued in 1864 and 1865, from designs by C. H. Bennett, are reproduced here, it is possible that other candidates might put forward reasonable claims. It seems probable that ornamented note paper and envelopes appeared just before the cards, that the designs in relief, identical with those on the stationery named, were either simultaneously or very shortly after stamped in the centre of a card, which had its edges coloured or embossed. Certain it is that T. Sulman was very early in the field with relief-decorated paper and cards, and with lithographed designs. Leighton, of Fleet Street, and Mansell, of Red Lion Square, are also amongst the first, while R. Canton, (who started Valentine and Birthday card production in 1840,) and Dean & Sons issued many of their publications with special Christmas mottoes. The innovation of stamping reliefs in two or more colours is dated to 1858. The introduction of foreign "chromo-lithograph pictures," to replace those hitherto coloured by hand, or by stencil, is traced to Elliott, of Bucklesbury, in 1850, and to Scheffer and Scheiper, (I have but the phonetic spelling of these names,) in 1851. This item in the preparation of "made-up" Birthday Cards and Valentines had hitherto been very rudely prepared by colouring plain embossed relief with a brush, or stencilling lithographs, afterwards embossed and cut out. An improvement in these devices is traced to a man whose professional occupation was to colour designs upon linen bands for the Irish trade. These cut out devices were prepared at a cost of 4d. per 1,000, the hands earning about 15s. a week, until Germany sent over more cheaply produced imitations at one-sixteenth of the cost. Thierry, of Fleet Street, known as the father of the Christmas card trade, was, doubtless, the first to introduce the elaborately embossed reliefs which afterwards came over in cart loads. Then they cost 80s. per 100 sheets, now their price has fallen to 1s. the 100 for large quantities. When one remembers that at first and for many years after a large majority of the cards, (which, however little they interest us here, helped to spread the fashion), were made up from foreign chromo-lithographs, even by firms of the high standing of Marcus Ward, we find that this importation of foreign embossed relief takes its place as an important commercial factor in the rise of the industry.

Without dwelling too long on the growth of the manufacture of cards in England, it may be interesting to record a few facts obtained chiefly from Mr Jonathan King, who has followed the subject, from inside knowledge, more closely, perhaps, than any other living person. His collection, contained in some 700 volumes, weighing, collectively, between six and seven tons, includes about 163,000 varieties, and although not exhaustive (as indeed might be safely affirmed

KATE GREENAWAY — M. W. AND CO.

of any collection of any subject), offers what is practically a completely illustrated history of the many years between 1862 and to-day. From the beginning we find types that recur again and again, and in not a few instances the early specimens are more satisfactory than the revivals, despite the increased mechanical perfection which marks the products of recent date. This "jewelling," a feature to-day, may be traced to the old "tinsel" ornaments used for embellishing theatrical portraits. A unique collection of these punched-out devices, in brilliant metallic colours, is said to be in the possession of Mr Harry Furniss. The perforated borders of 1894 are foreshadowed by the devices of the fifties and sixties; the "illuminated" style, which distinguished the best years of the "Marcus Ward" cards, are anticipated by most excellent specimens in 1867 and 1868 in T. Sulman's sample books, some of which are remarkably good in their close following of the best mediæval originals keeping the spirit of the old missal, and much of its gorgeous colour, although in no way reproducing the quaint drawing or archaic devices of the originals. Two "love cards" by T. Sulman, Mr King considers to have been, very probably, the true ancestors of the Christmas card; he also attributes to the celebrated "Bagster" colour-prints of 1862, no little influence on the fashion which developed almost simultaneously. And for another possible ancestor he would place the illustrated sheets of note paper issued by Rock Bros., which include sketches by (or closely after) John Leech, of typical Christmas subjects, snowed-up party-goers and the like. Rixon & Arnold, of the Poultry, are said to have been the first to offer Christmas cards to retail purchasers. The frosting, introduced by King, in 1867, has constantly re-appeared; it is not a natural crystal, but a composition made from fine glass blown into thin bubbles and burst; the "jewelling," referred to above, is a thin film of copper faced with various chemicals and heated. Parker, who painted the linen bands for the Irish trade, is said to have been the first person to use jewels on cards. Natural grass and sea-weed, dried flowers, chenille, velvet, and crewel work, gelatine, and divers substances, unorthodox, and, as I think, reprehensible on the card, are no modern innovations, but have their precedents dating back a quarter of a century and more. But these few jottings must suffice, or the anecdotes of the card alien to the purpose of this sketch will crowd out matter more pertinent.

KATE GREENAWAY — M. W. AND CO.

Some firms have, evidently, from the very first set themselves the one task of selling; with these we need not be concerned here; nor with the large number of makers who delight in producing imitations of unlovely objects, luggage labels, cork soles, slices of blankets or of bacon, burnt ends of cigars, extracted teeth, and other horrors reproduced in realistic

W. F. YEAMES, R.A. R. T. AND S.

number of the specimens he has raked together from all sources.

Of Messrs Charles Goodall and Sons, who produced, in 1862, the series of cards which may be taken as the very earliest instance of their general use, I have already spoken. Despite the large number of impressions of the little embossed designs after Mr John Leighton ("Luke Limner," referred to on another page) and the fact that the production of these Christmas greetings would seem to an outsider to accord so well with their staple industry of playing-cards, and, notwithstanding that they were the solitary publishers at first, in a comparatively short time they abandoned the industry to other makers. Yet their share was all important, for they followed up the series referred to on an earlier page, year by year, with a rapidly increasing number of designs. In 1866 the late Mr. Josiah Goodall commissioned Messrs Marcus Ward & Co., of Belfast, to lithograph, for his firm, a set of four designs by C. H. Bennett, and in the following year another set by the same hand. These, together with Luke Limner's border design of Holly, Mistletoe, and Robins, may be taken as the forerunners of the real Christmas card.

With Messrs Marcus Ward & Co., who started the production of Christmas cards as imitation to accompany a message of goodwill to their friends. Nor with those again who issue cards with fac-similes of coins, or cork-screws, razors or hairpins, in low coloured relief, for the sake of a punning legend underneath. These things, concrete practical jokes of the feeblest order, have their scheme in the economy of life perhaps, so doubtless have blackbeetles, earthquakes, fogs, and the omnipresent bacillus, but it is easy to forget them when they do not actively obtrude their unwelcome presence.

Few of those concerned in the beginning of the Christmas card guessed for a moment the huge popularity which awaited it. Hence they took no trouble to secure for themselves a complete set of their wares, duly annotated with information concerning the artist and his design. Their appreciation for any old design you will find is apt to be coloured by the amount of profit it earned. Hence the few that come back to their memory as triumphs are apt to be quite insignificant things; so trivial that if the name of their designer chances also to have escaped oblivion, it may be left to the limited immortality of the manufacturer's memory; or to be hunted up in future by some over-zealous collector who is omnivorous, and cares not a jot for the intrinsic merit of the items he collects, so that he may add to the

W. F. YEAMES, R.A. R. T. AND S.

early as 1867, coincidentally with the opening of their London house, however, we come to a very different class of manufacturers. Here is a house, one of the earliest in production, with a record that reaches the highest level of decorative excellence ever touched by the Christmas card. This firm for a while monopolised the whole of the better-class trade. Beginning with the use of German "chromos," usually mounted on card with lithographed borders in gold and colours, of home manufacture, they soon issued reproductions of original designs by artists of repute, and gained a position where they stood without rivals. It was, I believe, owing to the acute perception of one of the partners of this firm, Mr. William H. Ward, that Miss Kate Greenaway was "discovered" as a designer. At the earliest "Black and White" Exhibition at the Dudley Gallery Mr. Ward's attention was drawn to Miss Greenaway's work; and recognising that her special talent was in the direction of costume figures and dainty colours, he induced her to design for the firm. The pictures that were thus indirectly responsible for the long series of cards reflected equal credit on the artist and the firm who produced them. The drawings themselves Sprites, Gnomes, and Fairies were bought by the Rev. W. J. Loftie, who then edited the *People's Magazine*, in which woodcut reproductions of them were

H. R. STEER H. AND F.

notable artists who designed for tuis firm, during issued. Later on mention is made of other the years of its supremacy. But times changed, other firms entered the field, some worthy foemen, others pandering to the vulgar taste, until, after many years, although Messrs Marcus Ward and Co. have not entirely abandoned the manufacture, they have retired from any serious attempt to compete with the quantity of patterns, mostly "made in Germany," which flood the market. It is worth noting that Germany begins and ends the great period of popularity. Once cheapness is set against quality, the English are beaten. This does not imply that German cards are necessarily poor in design or execution. Probably at no period was mechanical excellence more faultless than as to-day, when scarce one design in a thousand has any but the slightest artistic interest. But the low-priced German labour forced the English makers to reduce the prices they paid their artists, and so ultimately they ceased to control the industry.

The sample books of this firm, which would present a most honourable record of intelligent progress, have, unfortunately, been destroyed, or to be more accurate, survive only in portions. Yet even in the imperfect evidence they offer, one sees proof that the fame it achieved was deserved. When Mr Andrew Lang wrote in his *Arts' Martyr*

[illegible] H. AND F.

"Such awful colours as are blent
On terrible placards,
Where flames the fierce advertisement,
Yea; or on Christmas cards
(Not Ward's,
But common Christmas cards)."

the choice of the surname of the producer, if explained by the neat rhyme it offers, is also fully justified by sober fact. For in the "Marcus Ward" cards, especially in the middle or later periods, there is sign of one consistent supervision—and this undoubtedy is largely, if not wholly, traceable to the presence of Mr Thomas Crane in the firm as director of its department of design. This artist, brother to Mr Walter Crane, had the courage to send out to a public that, again and again, shows its indifference to "conventional" design, a series of cards which—quite apart from the excellence of their pictures, or floral devices were embellished by most refined and appropriate ornamentation on their borders and backs. The lettering was not left to chance, or reduced to the bare simplicity of a label in ordinary type, obviously an addition to the design, but was planned to accord with it. The colours which distinguish this class of decoration are unusually happy. Pale blue lettering on sage green ground, citrons, olives, and tertiary colours were employed much as they were used by the so-called æsthetic school of furnishers of the same period. Without being unduly "precious," or confined to esoteric symbolism

A. LUDOVICI, JUNR. H. AND F.

and "Grosvenor-gallery" figures, they did attempt to observe the canons of conventional design. From the year 1873, when Mr H. Stacy Marks, R.A., issued through this firm the only set of cards he has designed, we find examples of work that may be second-rate when set beside the best examples of missals and other mediæval decoration, but are not unworthy to be considered with them. For in the best of these cards the limitations within which coloured printing can alone hope to be self-sufficient are duly observed.

A. LUDOVICI, JUNR. H. AND F.

As in Japanese art the convention of a bold, arbitrary outline is accepted so also is the use of flat colour, and a purely decorative shading that does not for an instant seek to imitate nature. Or, on the other hand, when pictures are introduced and the realism of pictorial art is observed, then similar reticence prevails; very rarely is there an attempt to conceal the fact that it is a printed and not a painted picture which is itself usually surrounded by a frame work, serving to carry the lettering, and to present it in a setting that makes the whole complete. Contrasting these cards with those of other makers, whose chief effort is to imitate a little picture, without the slightest attempt to make the card itself a decorative and complete design, we can but regret that fashion soon grew tired of this style, and influenced, no doubt, by the vignetted landscapes with floral details stuck

E. BLAIR LEIGHTON H. AND F.

around it, which the American magazines were never tired of introducing in their pages, was satisfied with the merely pretty. The one ideal is that of a panel, duly bordered and self-contained, the other a leaf of a sketch book, with a landscape or a figure piece, more or less surrounded by natural flowers or foliage. At one time it was the fashion for any apostles of reform to illustrate their argument by "horrid examples." In the early days of what is now South Kensington Museum, a room was set aside as a chamber of horrors, but it was found that the public eagerly accepted new vices they had hitherto shunned only from ignorance of their existence. Hence the practice has fallen out of favour, and I am forbidden to illustrate here many too popular specimens of the class of work which supply the antithesis to the Marcus Ward ideal. Yet, at the risk of reiterating what has been already said, it must be pointed out that the high praise which these cards (as it seems to me) deserve is not so much for their own excellence as for their recognition of the true ideal of applied art, and their efforts to induce the public to accept something that recognised law, and the beauty of ordered taste, instead of a lawless caprice which ignores precedents, and itself does not assist in forming [illegible] for future workers to observe.

It is this characteristic which must be reckoned to the honour of Marcus Ward's cards; not because they employed celebrated artists more freely than other firms—capable designers indeed were commissioned, but their list of well-known painters will not compare in mere numbers for a moment with those of several of their near rivals—but because they saw that an architectural, not a pictorial, aim was the correct one. To talk of architecture in connection with so ephemeral an object as a Christmas card may sound absurd, but, nevertheless, I think all students of decoration must admit that its treatment should be more nearly allied to the surface decoration of buildings than to transcripts of nature, which are, in theory, attempts to imitate the out-look from a window of the building. This latter, usually held to be the aim of the pictorial artist, cannot be employed without degradation upon mechanically-produced reproductions in colour; but the artificial convention—the idea of decorative as distinguished from pictorial art—wherever you find it for stained glass, mosaic, enamel, inlay or colour printing, has another purpose to fulfil, which is more admirably achieved when the limitations of the material are duly observed.

E. BLAIR LEIGHTON H. AND F.

"WHAT CHEER," FROM AN ETCHING BY A. H. HAIG, R.P.E.

F. MARKHAM SKIPWORTH H. AND F.

Of the artists who designed for Marcus Ward's publication, the most prominent are: H. Stacy Marks, R.A., Walter Crane, Miss Kate Greenaway, Miss A. M. Lockyer, Percy Tarrant, Henry Rylands, E. J. Ellis, S. T. Dadd, Patty Townshend, H. Arnold, Fred Miller, Moyr Smith, Thomas Goodman, and Thomas Crane.

Among the early cards issued about 1875, a few sets deserve noting. One of "*The Nativity,*" four cards in gold and colours, was probably designed by Goodman. Several sets, "*Christmas in the Olden Time,*" figures against a gold background, are by Moyr Smith; a somewhat similar set is probably by R. Dudley. A clever series, verses with borders of asparagus and red berries, must not be forgotten. To this period belong also many embossed designs in gold and colours, that are curiously near the style so popular at the present time, when to secure a jewelled effect seems the aim of every firm. Those issued in, or after 1878, include a very clever imitation of a Japanese lacquer cabinet, with folding doors, by T. Walter Wilson, some excellent sets of flowers in natural colours, on cleverly treated Japanese diaper patterns, in gold and silver, by Tarrant. There are two of these sets, with four designs in each, and a similar set in blue and white. The patterns of the background, although based on Japanese art, appear to have been exercises in the style of Japan, not transcripts of genuine patterns. The many studies of children by Percy Tarrant cannot be enumerated here most, if not all, bear his initials or signature, so that their identification is easy. A noticeable design produced by this firm was issued in one pattern only a fairly large card, with the centre covered by four flaps, each bearing on the inner side a fairy on a spray of flowers against a blue sky with moon. A set of graceful heads in monochrome by Alfred Ward, and designs by Walter Crane, Thomas Crane, and Kate Greenaway, described elsewhere, belong to this time. A set by Henry Ryland of *Angels of the Nativity*, should be mentioned; also some decorative subjects, and others with bric-à-brac well drawn and printed upon thick cards, with black and gold lacquer backs. A set of reproductions of water-colour drawings of *Cottages*, by Patty Townshend; a set of *Heads*, by Edwin J. Ellis; some of S. T. Dadd's clever *Animal Studies;* a very popular series, with designs of ferns in perforated blue and white china pots, on peacock green background; cards simulating an open envelope containing sprays of flowers; a clever folding card, with kittens climbing a ladder against a brick wall, and a conventional sprig of holly in pale olive on a blue-green ground, for its outer cover; a bold set of *Hunting Sketches*, by Miss G. Bowers, not unlike Caldecott's; and many others can only be hastily noted. It is pleasant to observe that from the first the products of this firm are full of decorative interest. The

H. AND F.

technical excellence is no less marked; and no doubt much of this was due to the supervision of Mr. W. H. Ward.

A collection of original drawings, chiefly for Christmas cards, prepared for their publications, were sold by Fosters, in 1884, for £1,798 12s, two sets by Miss Greenaway fetching ten guineas each.

No space can be given here for a notice of its booklets, calendars, or valentines, although the latter include some charming designs by Kate Greenaway, and a set by Walter Crane that is, perhaps, the most delightful group of all his many printed fancies. Valentines, Easter cards, and the like, were, in Messrs Ward's hands, imbued with the same fancy that raised the Christmas card to a better position — but they, too, failed to survive the influx of inanity which again conquered the field of St. Valentine.

Messrs De la Rue must needs occupy a very prominent place in any record of the Christmas Card movement. They entered the field in 1875, and, excepting possibly a few of the very earliest, possess a complete set of their samples from 1876 to 1885, when they abandoned the publication of Christmas cards. Their work throughout is distinguished by a high degree of mechanical excellence and by great fertility of idea, and one or two of the most notable departures in designs — the classical figures of nude children, for instance — can be traced to their initiation. The list of well-known artists who designed for them is singularly large. They faithfully accepted what must needs remain the purist's ideal of a Christmas card — a symmetrical, decorated panel, complete in itself, and treated usually within a framework bearing

R. DUDLEY — D. L. R. AND CO.

R. DUDLEY — D. L. R. AND CO.

R. DUDLEY — D. L. R. AND CO.

R. J. ABRAHAM R. T. AND CO.

the legend. The thousand and one subjects, heretofore deemed unseasonable, that they introduced on their cards, bear witness to the amount of thought bestowed upon their preparation; at the same time, it must be urged against them that this catholicity proved fatal, in the end, to the theoretical fitness of the card for its purpose. Even *Punch*, not often interested in such matters, was provoked to a pictorial parody of their lightly-clad maidens shivering in the sleet of a typical English December. Compared, however, with the licence indulged in by other firms, Messrs De la Rue and Marcus Ward stand out distinct, if not entirely alone, as the "classical" publishers, who withstood the vulgar demand for novelty at any price; and when the taste for meretricious rubbish grew more and more evident, relinquished the attempt to rival their opponents on their own ground. This must not, however, be taken as any slight cast on Messrs Raphael Tuck & Co., S. Hildesheimer & Co., Hildesheimer & Faulkner, Ernest Nister and the rest. New ideals arose, and new efforts were made to raise the art of the card with marked success in a hundred instances. But these ideals, as a rule, were satisfied with facsimile reproduction of drawings by well-known artists, and were only by accident Christmas cards. A change of lettering had made them equally suitable for Birthday, or Easter greetings a change of substance, paper for card, and the majority would be equally well adapted for book illustration. Messrs De la Rue, however, clung loyally to that idea of the card, which I have elsewhere considered to be ruled by architecture, rather than painting; and although it would be folly to say that every design they issued, if enlarged, might fitly take its place as a decorative panel in a building—yet by way of indicating broadly the difference between the schools of decorative art and naturalistic art, some such rough and ready test can be successfully applied to their work, speaking of it as a whole.

As, by the courtesy of the firm, their books have been available for reference for the preparation of this article, it will be easy to give a rapid summary of the most noticeable cards, in the order of their production. In the series for Christmas, 1876, the most striking are a set of *Landscapes*, by Miss J. M. Dealy; some clever

R. J. ABRAHAM R. T. AND CO.

ALICE HAVERS H. AND F.

reproductions of *Japanese Drawings*, and a comic series by Ernest Griset the quaint delineator of animal life; also many designs by Aubert, a pupil of Owen Jones, who contributed largely to the general decoration of Messrs De la Rue's cards; and some others, probably by Alfred Hunt. In 1877, we find designs by G. C. Kilburne, Ernest Griset, and others. In 1878 appears a series of *Classical Studies*, by W. S. Coleman, the first of the many daintily drawn figures of children nude, or slightly draped, which won such enormous popularity; *Youthful Beauties, Blowing Bubbles*, are other sets, this year, by the same artist. E. H. Fahey's *Message of the Cross*, three rich and very harmonious designs, are all of this date. In 1879, W. S. Coleman is represented by a *Harvest of Beauty, Sylvan Sports, Cupids, Gardens, Nymphs, Eastern Damsels, and Youthful Graces*. A set of *Divers*, and *Old English Games* by a forgotten artist, are noticeable for their vigour. The *Finger Shadows*, and *Marionettes*, both by E. H. Fahey, and *Liliputians*, by G. C. Kilburne, belong to this year. In 1880, a very charming set of oblong cards, by Robert Dudley, *War of the Roses*, is a typical example of an artist of considerable reputation in other fields. Here again we find W. S. Coleman, with *Girlish Delights, Jocund Youth, Dancing Girls*, and others, always issued in sets containing three designs each.

To this year belongs the series of *Little Maidens* by Rebecca Coleman—highly finished heads of children, printed in the best style of chromo-lithography. Two sets by Major Seccombe, whose illustrations of military life had a somewhat extended reputation at this period, entitled, *In the Clouds*, and *The Tournament*; a set of *Mermaids*, by Kilburne; a set of *Squirrels*, by Gordon Browne; and a set of *Fisher Lads*, by Miss Coleman, are also in the same book. In 1881, we find a really beautiful set, entitled, *Ariel*, by Robert Dudley, from figures typifying *Earth, Air, Fire, and Water*, some of which are illustrated on page 21. W. S. Coleman is represented by several series, *In the Shade, By the Pool, Swinging Figures*, and *Shell Gatherers*; Rebecca Coleman has a series, *Sunbeams*; a set named *The Lovers' Creed*, by J. Lawson, is also noticeable.

The album of samples for 1882 includes two striking sets, *The Magician* and *Cupid's Garden*, by Robert Dudley; *The Bathers*, by W. S. Coleman; and *Japanese Belles*, pretty studies of little *musumé*, by Rebecca Coleman.

ALICE HAVERS H. AND F.

ALICE HAVERS H. AND F.

In 1883, we find two *Grecian Studies*, by F. S. Walker, who then did much illustration for contemporary periodicals, but is now better known by his contributions to the Royal Society of Painter-Etchers, of which he is a member. Robert Dudley has a very graceful group *Garlands of the Year:* a set, *The Village Church*, is good, but the artist cannot be identified now; *Reposing*, by J. Lawson, is also one of the most noteworthy of this year.

The selection of patterns for 1884-5, is less noticeable; it contains *The Arts*, by Robert Dudley; *Youthful Studies* and *Soap Bubbles*, by W. S. Coleman; *Little Folks*, by J. Lawson; and some clever studies of animals *Home Favourites*, by an artist I have been unable to identify.

This brief summary of Messrs De la Rue's important share in the publication of Christmas cards is limited chiefly to a consideration of figure subjects, by artists whose reputation has been won, for the most part, in the orthodox way. Nearly all the names here quoted are those of regular exhibitors in art galleries. Mr. W. S. Coleman, as the painter of several of the large and admirably reproduced pictures issued with *Pears' Annual*, is familiar to thousands who have long since forgotten his Christmas cards. The very small number of landscapes and flowers they issued, compared with the quantity of figure subjects, is worth recording, as elsewhere the reverse almost invariably obtains.

Messrs Eyre & Spottiswoode, who, beginning in 1879, for a time published cards which deserve some amount of attention, are unable to supply any information of their products. Nor, so far as their sample books (which I have been able to inspect) elsewhere show, did they ever initiate any noticeable departure. Good taste, with no striking individuality to distinguish their publications from those of the best of their contemporaries may be a fair verdict to give hastily. In 1881, a series by Frank Feller, of *Sportsmen, Sailors and Policemen*, and two figures in the style of H. S. Marks, R.A., were possibly their most popular patterns. In 1883, a series of

H. AND F.

Inquisitive Pigs, by Irene Brindley, deserve a word of approval. A catalogue of original drawings belonging to this firm, sold by auction in 1887, includes many by Frank Feller, Elizabeth Folkhard, C. M. Jessop, T. R. Kennedy, Bertha Maguire, J. Proctor, Percy Tarrant, A. H. Warren, Linnie Watt, and Annette Whymper,—nearly all names of artists who prepared designs for most of the popular houses of the period.

That the firm of Raphael Tuck & Co. does not occupy far more space in these pages is due, first to the enormous quantity of its publications making anything like a complete record however slightly done impossible, and, next to the fact that it has not kept for reference even a series of its catalogues, much less a complete set of all its thousands of publications. Even Mr King's collection does not include (I believe) all the various items published by this house, which issued large numbers of patterns, until, in 1881, we find one hundred and eighty sets, representing seven hundred designs in its sample books for that year alone. The previous year, 1880, the firm held an exhibition of designs for Christmas cards, opened on October 28th, at the Dudley Gallery, Egyptian Hall; £500 was given in prizes. The judges, Sir Coutts Lindsay, H. S. Marks, R. A., and G. H. Boughton, A.R.A., selected a number of the 925 designs exhibited, and afterwards the firm chose, according to their knowledge and experience, a great many more. It is needless to say, in view of the opinion I have expressed elsewhere on the power of the middleman in art, that the sale of the cards was almost entirely in the inverse ratio of their artistic position those which gained high prizes selling but fairly well, even at the best, while many of those passed over by the judges proved extremely popular designs. The moral of this anecdote is too obvious to need comment. The chief prizes reproduced for the season 1881-2, were as follows: Alice Squire, 1st prize, £100, for a set of children in landscapes poppies are conspicuous in one of the cards; 2nd prize, Thomas Herbert

ALICE HAVERS H. AND F.

Allchin, for floral subjects; 3rd prize, H. M. Bennett, for the Seasons, figures with sunflowers, etc.; and Patty Townshend, for *Children in Snow*; 4th prize, May S. Story, for a set of birds and flowers; 5th prize, R. J. Abraham, for two admirable classic designs of figures (reproduced on page 22); 6th prize, K. Terrell, for designs after the style of Kate Greenaway; 7th prize, Rebecca Coleman, for a set of *Angels' Heads*, which almost broke the record for popular success; Helen J. Miles, for a series of circular panels of figures on square gold background; George Clausen, the well-known artist, for two pastorals, *Shepherds*, etc., issued as a folding card, with charmingly decorated exterior; Kate Sadler, for finely-coloured studies of roses; Marian Croft, for some dainty children; and E. A. Bailey, for studies of owls. In the following year, 1882-3, commissions were given to several Royal Academicians. Here, again, artistic fame and the approval of fellow-artists did not go on all fours with the suffrages of the great public; and one finds that the commercial success of these cards is not comparable with that achieved by a comparatively unknown artist, or with the insignificant efforts of nobody in particular. Even when the subjects were so similar, and the artistic treatment hardly different, the *Angels' Heads*, by J. Sant, R.A., did not hit the public taste like those by Rebecca Coleman. It would seem, in this instance, as if, two designs of equal merit being offered, the public preferred the work of the outsider to that of the honoured member of the Royal Academy. The "R.A." series included two *Angels with Harps*, by the late J. C. Herbert, R.A., for which silence is the only polite comment; a set of four *Children in Snow*, not typical of Marcus Stone, R.A., their author; single seated figures, by G. D. Leslie, R.A., also lacking the naïve charm of his oil paintings; a

ALICE HAVERS H. AND F.

ALICE HAVERS H. AND F.

series of Christmas subjects, *Children Decorating the Home*, with holly, etc., by W. C. T. Dobson, R.A., which are, in many respects, the nearest approach to entirely suitable designs in the whole group; two compositions by E. J. Poynter, R.A., somewhat in the style of his well-known insurance advertisement, and singularly ineffective in their reproductions; the afore-mentioned *Angels' Heads*, by J. Sant, R.A., very pleasant and graceful designs; some clever studies of *Caged Cupids*, by W. T. Yeames, R.A., (page 15) with really charming decoration in pale colours upon the outer sides of the folding cards on which they were printed; and several of children's faces by J. C. Horsley, R.A. But speaking of the whole series, whether the designs failed in their reproduction whether they were designed on too large a scale, and lost by diminished size, or whether the authors tried to be too pictorial, is not easy to say, yet, if the above criticism be just, it will be seen that the successes and failures were alike unexpected. The men one had thought would make a capital Christmas card lost their gaiety and sprightly charm, and became merely dull; others, more serious in their routine work, came nearer to scoring successes.

It would seem that to commission an artist to go out of his way and prepare a scheme for work outside his sympathy is nearly always fatal. The music made to order for state festivals and exhibition openings, the decoration planned by picture painters, the criticism written at an editor's request by novelists — one might extend the list indefinitely — is usually entirely unrepresentative, and rarely indeed even a *succès d'estime*. Hence, the fact that the Royal Academy was commissioned to revolutionize the art of the Christmas card, and failed even to divert its current for a year, need not gladden its foes or depress its friends. The card industry, susceptible as it was to the veriest trifle — such as a black background, or a slightly new convention in landscape vignettes — remained unmoved; the public also remained unmoved; and if the stock did not follow the example of

ALICE HAVERS H. AND

ALICE HAVERS — H. AND F.

the manufacturers and public, it was probably because the former knew the taste of the latter too well to risk very large editions of any of these designs. To Messrs Raphael Tuck & Co. due praise must be given; to whom should they go for an advance on a public competition if not to the official body at the head of English Art? No doubt, if the comparatively few Academicians and Associates (at that period) who showed a taste for decorative, as opposed to pictorial, art had consented to enter the lists—cards by the President, L. Alma Tadema, R.A., Sir John Millais R.A. (fancy his children as cards!)—to take a few at random, not heeding whether they were Associates or full blown R.A.'s at the given date—would have left notable examples; as it is, one surveys the much advertised series with frigid [illegible], and only praises the firm for its pluck in carrying the scheme through.

Among other notable cards issued by this firm, some by Louisa, Marchioness of Waterford—the extremely facile artist, of whom both Watts and Landseer are reported to have said she was "the first amateur in Europe"—are sure to be prized; especially the designs, the one, children in a gallery, with oranges; the other, a child in a long white frock, with pages holding her train—all in Carolean costume. A clever series of monochrome studies, *Presented at Court*, by H. Sandier, and many sets of etchings deserve more notice than can be given here.

Nor can we devote space here to the fine reproductions of Raphael's pictures issued by this firm. A collector will find more of Raphael Tuck's publications essential to complete his selection of typical cards, than any other single firm can offer; and, at the same time, he will find those "he has no use for," to employ an American idiom, are as likely to bear the

W. S. COLEMAN — D. L. R. AND CO.

W. S. COLEMAN D. L. R. AND CO.

well-known trade mark of Raphael Tuck & Co. as that of any less known firm.

In the earliest, as in all the later products of Messrs Hildesheimer & Faulkner, the dominant influences that show, are what one may call "popular academic," rather than "aesthetic," taste; that is to say, their bias has been toward pictorial, rather than purely decorative treatment. Speaking generally of these publications, the interest centres in the picture; but one may readily admit that, having chosen this form of art, they spared no effort to do it full justice. Yet, as a peculiarly sane art-critic said of late, when discussing the qualities of posters: "They should not attempt any emulation of the subject picture; such attempts look vulgar and cheap, instead of effective; because they pretend to subtleties and qualities foreign to their nature. A good poster is not a bad imitation of something else, but a separate work of art, in which lines, tints, or whatever may be used, are in themselves interesting, as well as effectively combined." Applied to cards in place of posters, this criticism expresses the only objection worth sustaining against the majority of the cards of the eighties, as opposed to those of the seventies. One may grant, for purposes of argument, that those of the later decade are better drawn, better printed, and better finished, and yet feel that all this expenditure of taste, technique and mechanism, is to be regretted when one bears in mind the results which had been found possible while working strictly on the lines of the original designers.

To return, however, to the cards of Messrs Hildesheimer & Faulkner (now C. W. Faulkner & Co.). Before 1880, nothing is preserved, but in that year flowers by Mrs Duffield; some *Floral Studies*, by W. J. Muckley; *Figures*, by George Sadler; *Children*, by E. K. Johnson; *Kittens*,

W. S. COLEMAN D. L. R. AND CO.

W. S. COLEMAN D. L. R. AND CO.

by H. H. Couldery; a *Circus* series, and other half-comic designs, by A. Ludovici, Junr.; and others by G. C. Kilburne, show that they had already allied themselves with artists, to be identified for many years with their productions, and had definitely set themselves their own standard of excellence. In this year and the next, 1881, flowers, by Mrs Duffield and W. J. Muckley, predominate; but among figure painters then new to the public, Jane M. Dealy is represented by several sets of *Children*, full of a quaintly naïve charm of their own. E. K. Johnson has also several clever *Studies of Children*. Some good *Boat Subjects* are contributed by C. Davison, and E. Manby has popular *Studies of Heads*. A. Ludovici, Junr., appears with several sets,

W. S. COLEMAN D. L. R. AND CO.

W. S. COLEMAN D. L. R. AND CO.

Cyclists, *Street Arabs*, etc., being the most noticeable. Two really notable series of *Children*, designed by Carl Gregory, stand out prominently, both for their excellent composition and admirable drawing. H. H. Couldery contributes nine of his charming *Kittens;* but recalling Ruskin's criticism of one of his Academy pictures for 1875—"Quite the most skilful piece of minute and Dureresque painting in the exhibition (it cannot be rightly seen without a lens), and in its sympathy with kitten nature down to the most appalling depths thereof, and its tact and sensitiveness to the finest gradations of kittenly meditations and motion—unsurpassable"—one realises instantly the gulf which yawns between the best chromo-lithograph and the original painting. It seems to me the study of one of Couldery's cards—side by side with the picture Mr Ruskin's criticism brings back to memory—suffices to prove what I have tried to insist upon (over tediously, I fear) in this discursive survey of Christmas cards—the superiority of conventional to pictorial treatment for this particular purpose.

In 1882, Messrs Hildesheimer & Faulkner instituted a Prize Competition; the work sent in was hung at the galleries of the Society of British Artists in Suffolk Street (not then "Royal") and judged by Messrs J. E. Millais, R.A. and Marcus Stone, R.A. £5,000 was the amount of the prizes offered, and this, as receipts still extant show, was actually paid in sums

W. S. COLEMAN D. L. R. AND CO.

W. S. COLEMAN D. L. R. AND CO.

varying from £250, downwards. Miss Alice Havers took the first prize for *A Dream of Patience*—a card, portions of which are illustrated here. The outer panels of the folding triplicate card were decorated effectively with panels of sunset skies, and flowers. To E. K. Johnson was awarded the second prize of £150, for *Two Figures*, which are also reproduced here. It was a notable year for the firm, despite the fact that the enterprise, like other bold undertakings, failed to compensate the projectors immediately; although looking back at it now, they realise that ultimately it proved to have been indirectly a financial as well as a direct artistic success. The "*Patience*" card cost over £750 before a copy was printed, and

W. S. COLEMAN D. L. R. AND CO.

THOMAS CRANE M. W. AND CO.

perfection in some cases; but, on the whole, the work done in so short a time deserves warm approbation. It would serve no purpose to record the list of prizes here, or to distinguish the designs thus honoured from those commissioned in the ordinary way. In the book for Christmas, 1882, are many *Studies of Children*, by Jane Dealy—showing great advance upon her first efforts; some graceful *Landscape Vignettes*, by Ernest Wilson, the first publication of a young artist, whose designs attained such wide popularity in after years, and whose career promised so much. W. J. Hodgson, now of *Punch*, also appears in this year's book. Mme Henriette Ronner has a series of *Cats*. Percy Tarrant is represented by his first published set of cards—one a figure of a jester in red motley the snow. Miss L. Watt, who took a high

THOMAS CRANE M. W. AND CO.

never quite repaid its cost; yet even to-day, if we were asked to name the best English card of the modern style, it would come to mind for hasty quotation, and one is not sure whether any amount of reflection would oust it from the place of honour. Many of the prize winners became regular contributors to the future books of the firm, and a number of their works were issued for the following Christmas trade. The hasty production of these, necessary by force of circumstance, caused the results to fall short of

M. W. AND CO.

prize, has some of her graceful studies of children; Alfred Ward is represented by four charming heads in red monochrome; E. Blair Leighton has two figure subjects; Octavius Rickatson, then a clever student of the Royal Academy, contributes two sets of broadly treated landscapes, which suffered much in reproduction; H. W. Batley, the well-known designer, has an interesting set; A. W. Cooper, J. Mc L. Ralston, Margery May, J. Stephens, Sandier, and Mme Dubourg, are each represented. Mrs Staples (M.E.E.), has some most dainty studies of child-life. A. Ludovici contributes some clever satirical sketch of *Æsthetes*, then in the time of *Patience*, the favourite butts for mild ridicule. Henry Reynolds Steer has a very admirable set—*Musicians*. J. E. Barclay contributes several charming sets of flowers; and, to cut short a list

W. J. MUCKLEY H. AND F.

that might be commented upon *ad infinitum*, W. J. Muckley surpasses his record as a successful floral painter, by a series of flowers in vases, which also come into the charmed circle of the very best designs. In all the books of all the makers, few so consistently reach achievement as this said book for 1882.

In 1883, we find Mrs Staples (M.E.E.) with more delicately-painted children's figures; W. J. Hodgson, with many sets, all humourous *Athletics*, *Bed-time*, *Bucolics*, *Gardening*, *Pigs*, *Snowballing*, etc. Ernest Wilson, who was drowned at Dittisham on the Dart before the next year's cards appeared, is represented by more of his dainty foreground studies; Miss Folkhard contributes a clever set of heads; Reginald Jones, some capital landscapes; and St. Clair Simmons, a popular black and white artist to-day, a set of figures; Mrs Fellowes surpasses her former series of still life by another set, wherein a Japanese yellow "sprinkler" vase figures prominently; J. E. Barclay, the popular portrait painter of New York (an Englishman, then living in London) has a set of white flowers and crosses, which must needs take a place in the most popular twenty sets published in England, however chosen; and J. Mc L. Ralston, for a long time an illustrator to *Good Words* and other periodicals, has a skating set. Two delightful figures this year are probably by Fred Morgan. Alice Havers contributes a very charming series of fairies in mid-air (one of which is reproduced on page 23); and W. J. Muckley is represented by

W. J. MUCKLEY H. AND F.

several sets, one of blue jars with white Japanese anemones, being peculiarly praiseworthy. The excellent semi-naturalistic convention of this painter of flowers, seen lately in one of Messrs Jefferies' wall papers, tempts even a partisan of purely conventional ornament to waive his theoretical objections, so that they do not exclude this clever artist.

In 1884, W. J. Hodgson (whose picture-book, the *Three Old Maids of Lee*, appeared about this time) contributes a quantity of comic cards, showing proof of that shrewd observation and power which won him afterwards a place on the staff of *Punch*. These include pictures of *Circus Life*, *Domestic Troubles*, *Curates*, *Skaters*, *Snowballing*, *Policemen*, etc. Ernest Wilson's *Landscapes*; S. T. Dadd's *Dogs and Squirrels*, etc.; E. K. Johnson's *Heads*; and pictures by Kilburne, are also noticeable. Alice Havers is responsible for a charming set of nude children in flower branches. A series of etchings *Low Tide*, *Barges*, etc., by Percy Robertson, also belonging to this year, are probably among the earliest published works by this clever son of a clever father.

ALFRED WARD H. AND F.

ALFRED WARD H. AND F.

In 1885, W. J. Hodgson is again to the fore with pictorial skits on *Lawn Tennis*, *Driving*, *Races*, and *Seaside Incidents*. B. D. Sigmund contributes several dainty landscapes; a set of swans and cascades deserve notice, although the identity of the signature is not quite clear; Jane Dealy has some pretty sketches of children in sun-bonnets, on the sands; Ernest Wilson's two series of landscapes, with meadow-sweet and other flowers in the foreground, and butterflies above, are possibly his best work, although some landscapes, with branches of gorse, wistaria, etc., in the foreground, come close to them for excellence in their own particular way. Alice Havers is represented by some dainty figures; F. C. Price, by *Seascapes* and *Sunsets*; Frank Feller, by designs of *Soldiers*.

In 1886, Jane Dealy is again to the front with *Sun-bonnetted Children* carrying babies; Miss Bennett has a tiny set of *Wee People*; Ernest Griset contributes sketches of *Skaters* and *Policemen*; Lizzie Lawson is represented by circular studies of *Heads*; F. Hines, by some capital landscapes; St. Clair Simmons, by children on palette-shaped panels; Mrs. Staples (M.E.E.) has several sets of *Children kneeling*, *At Church*, and *Guardian Angels*; J. Nelson Drummond's *Ships*; Alfred Bower's *Landscapes*; M. L. Gow's *Kneeling Children*; G. C. Fraser's *Landscape with Mills*; Jane Dealy's most popular set—*Three little Maids from School* (page 36); and T. Pyne's *Landscapes*, also deserve more detailed notice than can be given here. Alice Havers is largely and well represented—her kneeling, nude

ALFRED WARD H. AND F.

children, her ***Sleeping Children with Sprays of Flowers***, and the ***Madonna*** series, being especially good. F. Martin Skipworth, a painter who has since won high place, has several designs of ***Figures on a Sofa.***

In 1887, the artistic interest is fading somewhat. The mechanical excellence is as well sustained as ever, but the designs themselves are less individual. Floral arrangements naturalistically treated, and cards cut into all sorts of odd shapes, with trivial ornamentation, begin to usurp the whole field. Yet even at this time, a set of landscapes by the late Charles Robertson, of the Royal Society of Painter-etchers, and Royal Water Colour Society; a series of ***Boats***, by A. W. Weedon; a clever set of Indian children, by Jane Dealy; and Alice Havers' ***Angels with Doves***, and ***Shepherds***, stand out above the average. In 1889, a set by H. J. Stock, the painter of allegory and symbolic subjects, whose work is familiar at all the principal galleries, was the only one worth notice here. In 1890, a set by Charles Robertson may be mentioned. In 1891, a political set, by Bryan, the caricaturist portraits of Chamberlain, Churchill, and Gladstone, deserves mention as a unique instance (so far as I had then discovered) of politics being represented on Christmas cards. In 1891, a series by Alice Havers, ***Old Songs***, is really a reprint of some pages of a very charming volume published by the same firm.

The recent years are too close to need comment. But 1894 shows, in the special attention paid to capital photogravures of good pictures, that in another way art may again assert itself. That is to say, artists' pictures may be reproduced, more or less successfully, upon cards; but the difference between such a practice, and the designing of the whole card by an artist, is much wider asunder than the public guesses. Still, one is grateful for any indication of a wish for a higher ideal than that of a milliner or a maker of bon-bon boxes. The record of this firm proves as I tried to point out elsewhere that it is not always the manufacturer who should be blamed. When the public appreciate good design he is delighted to give it them; but if they will have nothing but petty trifles unless he can retire entirely from the manufacture, or turn his energies to other subjects -he must, for a while, like "Brer Rabbit," lie low, and hope for new allies to rout the champions of the common-place, who never cease their endeavour to drag down everything to their eminently respectable, but dull level of mediocrity, minute and uninteresting finish, and generally "pretty" ideal.

E. G. THOMSON D. L. R. AND CO.

Messrs Hildesheimer & Co. started publishing in 1876, with only two cards of their own make, the rest of their book being mainly foreign publications. In 1879, we find a large number of their own productions, chiefly flowers. Among these, a Japanese set is noticeable if only to

J. M. DEALY H. AND F.

show that, although almost every firm attempted to reproduce actual imitation of Japanese designs, they never succeeded in making the style the vogue even for a single season. This year, the abnormally popular design known to the trade as the "penny basket" was launched upon its long career. In 1880 or 1881 (the sample book includes both years), some long oblong cards, with blue beetles and other insects, will be recognised as a set that, oddly enough, achieved much appreciation. Another set of figures in landscapes obviously after Birket Foster were not, I think, designed by the artist for cards, but are adaptations of sketches made in the ordinary way. A set of four sea-pictures, possibly by Miss Whymper, are almost the only others of this year that are peculiarly noticeable; the chief subjects for 1879 to 1881, being arrangements of flowers. In 1882, we find evidence of the results of an Exhibition held in July, 1881, at St. James's Hall. The chief prize, £150, was taken by Linnie Watt, for some charming studies of children, in the style that made her so well known, and, if memory serves, won her no small reputation as a painter on china. One of the most original sets for this, or indeed for any year, consists of four studies of figures, by L. E. Lawrance, which, in their unconventional composition, recall Mr Alma Tadema.

In 1883, so far as the memory of those concerned can be trusted, the first set of Mr Wilfrid Ball's etchings was issued, followed, the next year, by two other sets—*Up Stream* and *Below Bridge*. By the courtesy of the artist, we are able to reproduce two examples from the first set. Probably no other Christmas cards ever published attained the dignity of being framed and treated seriously, as contributions to pictorial art, to the degree these etchings achieved it; or, if a few instances could be found, they are too rare to be mentioned in the same sentence. At the time it seemed as if half the rooms of cultured folk had at least one of these sets (usually arrayed in a gray French mount) framed in oak, and hung in a place of honour. There are also two other sets issued about this time—*Oxford* and *Cambridge*—by the same artist, whose reputation has been won in equal degree for his contributions to the galleries of the Painter-etchers, and the various water-colour exhibitions. One would not be surprised to find that the indirect reward for these dainty little things came in the form of almost instant fame. When a signature is attached to tens of thousands of copies of prints—carefully preserved and prized—

J. M. DEALY H. AND F.

W. T. BAXTER M. W. AND CO.

a draughtsman whose appreciation has hitherto been limited to artistic circles becomes a "man of the time" at once, with all the profits and penalties of the distinction.

To 1884 belongs a set of three booklets not memorable in themselves but probably the earliest examples of the booklet which was destined, in after years, to become so formidable a rival of the card. There were selections from *Pope*, *Thomson*, and *Burns*, with wrappers bearing portraits, in monochrome, of these poets, surrounded by wreaths.

In 1885, the sample books show several noticeable designs: one, a series of drawings of children, coloured in naturalistic fashion, against a lapis-lazuli background, whereon is a Dutch-metal landscape, in the fashion of a willow-pattern plate. This is, perhaps, the boldest flight into new fields of convention that can be discovered in the annals of the card. It fascinates the explorer into those regions of the past by its weird originality but, although it fascinates him, it fails to charm. A series of *Cats and Puppies*, decoratively treated; a set of Ernest Griset's designs; a very pleasant group, by Mrs Whymper, of beaches with breaking waves, and white sea-gulls hovering in silver skies, are the most noteworthy. But the card of the year, so far as the books of this firm are concerned, was undoubtedly Mr Wilfrid Ball's half-dozen miniature sketch-books, with alternate pages of manuscript and water-colour impressions in facsimile. The subjects are *Epping Forest*, *Burnham Beeches*, *Richmond*, *Hampton Wick*, *Windsor*, and *Putney*. The opening sentence on the first page of the latter takes away your breath as you read: "Mr Whistler, the foremost living etcher." Art criticism, sane, and at that time somewhat daring, employed when addressing the bourgeois patron, on a Christmas card! You pause, and cannot help wondering what was the result when the pleasant little essay was read out to bewildered breakfast tables in the suburbs, in the year of grace 1884; while you greatly applaud Mr Wilfrid Ball for his courageous attempt to gild a pill that the British public had not then learned to swallow as if they liked it. For, in sober truth, it is with a shock that one compares, even in fancy, the etchings thus brought to one's memory, and the whole array of cards, past and present, actually under notice. Fortunately, the *enfant terrible* who introduced so bold a statement himself may be regarded as one of the comparatively few instances of artists who have made us excellent cards or rather, who have produced charming designs as substitutes for the absolutely appropriate card. So, remembering his work and that of certain painters already mentioned here, one might feel less disturbed, were it not for the fact, which will insist on being recognised anew, that an etching, whether called a Christmas card or not, is, at least, an original work of art not a facsimile of one executed in another medium. Then the great division which sepa-

L. S. MATHER PRANG AND CO.

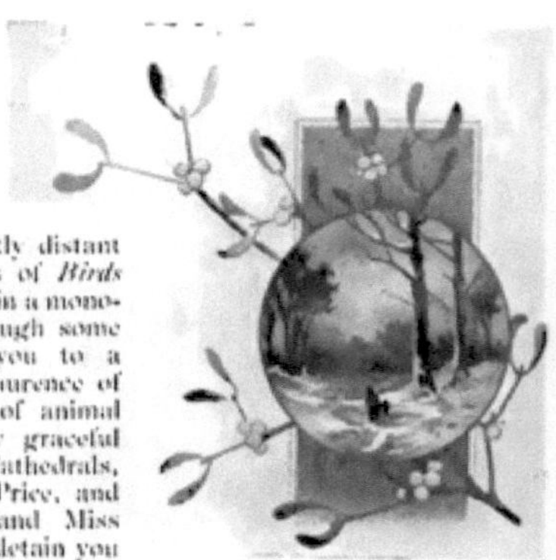

G. C. HAITÉ, R.B.A. M. W. AND CO.

rates so many of the applied arts of commerce, and the higher art, which must always suffer when reproduced by a meaner process, faces you. But the inevitable compromise between things as one would have them, and as circumstances permit them, is also seen clearly to be the only possible condition for safety.

So you pass on in a chastened view, and turn over the books for 1886, the last year sufficiently distant for free comment. There are some clever studies of *Birds* and *Kittens*, by C. E. G. The signature is arranged in a monogram, and the real name is not to be traced; although some capital landscapes with similar initials provoke you to a second attempt. B. B. L. obviously the B. B. Laurence of a former year, has some half-humourous studies of animal life. Wilfrid Ball is represented by sets of very graceful vignettes, facsimile water-colours; a set of English Cathedrals, signed F. P. B.; a series of landscapes by F. C. Price, and some by F. H. White; figures by Noel Smith and Miss Manning and Mr G. C. Haité's delightful landscapes detain you awhile; and, as you turn the last pages and see the shaped card and the other fanciful departures of the present day beginning to occupy much space, you feel the quest is over.

The most popular English patterns ever issued are naturally to be found in the cheapest cards S. Hildesheimer's historic "penny basket" set has already been mentioned; another card published, I believe, by Stevens of Coventry, printed by Jonas (?) and copied, if report be true, directly from an American design sold 500 gross by one publisher, and 5,000 (whether grosses or single cards is not said) by another firm. Why these simple studies of single birds against gold backgrounds should have been so extremely popular, is not easy to see. But no doubt other designs of quite insignificant cards were printed in huge numbers, since many are still in circulation on bon-bon boxes, cosaques, and similar goods– in addition to their legitimate use as cards.

Here where the whole 200,000 or so of Christmas cards have to be noticed in the most cursory fashion, it is not merely impossible to discuss the cards of other nations in a satisfactory manner, but even to mention any foreign cards, with a single exception. The publications of Messrs Prang, of Boston, cannot be ignored. Both for their intrinsic merits and the influence they had upon English taste, it is not easy, even now that their novelty has faded, to speak of them except in superlatives. For, with all due respect to our English makers, it is doubtful if any designs on this side of the Atlantic were better printed; indeed, it would be a somewhat difficult task to find a dozen examples published in England that could be set forward as worthy rivals to the best dozen of the Boston cards. Despite the claim several English firms are inclined to

S. H. AND CO.

L. B. HUMPHREYS PRANG AND CO.

enter for the honour of producing the first group or spray of coloured flowers against a solid black background. The craze which set in for this not very artistic arrangement undoubtedly may be traced to the American cards. Mr W. H. Ward, it seems, founded a branch of his firm in America, showing specimens of its work at the Centennial Exhibition, at Philadelphia. The success of the Marcus Ward cards, led Mr Louis Prang to produce the famous series, known all over the world.

Owing to the absence of a complete, authorized set of samples, and anything like a consecutive record of their products, I may be wrong in saying that Messrs Prang held a competitive exhibition of designs previous to our first experiment in that direction, which Messrs Raphael Tuck & Co. organized at the Dudley Gallery in 1880. Be that as it may, they had more than one such exhibition, as the prize cards (some of which are here reproduced by special permission) suffice to show. The $2,000 prize, taken by Dora Wheeler; the $1,000 prize awarded to Elihu Vedder, and other prize designs illustrated

PRANG AND CO.

were reproduced in sizes far larger than those usually adopted in England. The prices obtained for copies were also very much higher, so that it is hardly fair to set the results in direct competition with those produced for half, or quarter the cost on this side. But considering them apart from any comparison, how good they are! Not merely in design—as our black and white illustrations show—but in colour, they have, for the most part, a singular charm. Their designs are delicately finished without niggling detail, and the borders, lettering and backs, decorated with ornament which is never vulgar, and often peculiarly felicitous. Among other artists whose cards were issued by this firm, those by F. S. Mather, D. E. Whitney (charming flower studies); Léon Moran, G. Schackinger, Newton Mackintosh (a set of lettered panels on washes of broken colour, without other decoration, framed by a few broadly-designed flowers); Rose M. Sprague (dainty grotesque figures in flat colours, on plain backgrounds); Rosina Emmett (choristers); C. D. Weedon (children and flowers); L. B. Humphreys (sets of charming children in modern picturesque costume, and a single design *Coming out of Church*); Florence Taber and Alex. Sandier must needs be briefly mentioned. Two valentines by W. H. Low (probably issued also with Christmas greetings) are admirable examples of that most accomplished and graceful master.

E. K. JOHNSON — PRANG AND CO.

The charm of the colouring is not to be attributed entirely to a larger number of colour printings, or superior chromo-lithography; both these factors no doubt helped to give the peculiarly harmonious result; but one can feel beyond this, that the artists employed recognized from the first the limitation of all mechanical reproduction, however perfectly manipulated, and designed accordingly.

ROSINA EMMETT — PRANG AND CO.

Without championing the ideal of the Prang cards, which were often as un-Christmas-like in their subjects as most English cards; without claiming that their designs show in themselves more academic knowledge, more invention, or more graceful composition than our own—yet when you hunt for hours among the English sample books and unwittingly open a volume of these American cards, the chances are that it asserts itself, as distinctly more charming than the previous book, no matter whose you had chanced to be studying immediately before. It is painful to

PRANG AND CO

PRIZE CARD BY
WILL H. LOW.

ELIHU VEDDER. PRANG AND CO.

have to own so much, but, unfortunately, the conclusion is forced upon anyone who explores the vast stores of cards of the past for the purpose of discovering intrinsic beauty in the art set forth thereupon.

But that Mr Ernest Nister produced cards for publishers only until quite recently, and issued only booklets with his own imprint, it would be pleasant to speak in detail of his work. As the books for the last few years show, it is refined and dainty, with a very artistic treatment of the popular styles to-day. No books leave less opportunity for reproach, and one sees that if the higher ideal were once again restored to a genuinely artistic standard, here is a publisher ready to champion it. But buyers to-day appear

PRANG AND CO.

to be content to accept prettiness as the equivalent of beauty or, in other cases, to rush to the other extreme, and accept grotesque originality as the highest beauty. That Mr Aubrey Beardsley, Mr R. Anning Bell, and other distinguished artists to-day, have not (so far as I know) been asked to design a card, shows in itself that the industry is content to fall behind the taste of the moment, be it for good or evil. To blame any publisher for not sacrificing his profits by experimenting in new fields, were folly; did not one feel that even in this parlous state of the card, a bold venture might not merely renew its favour with educated people but possibly inaugurate a new era of appreciation. The latest movement in decorative art has not touched the card,

[illegible] PRANG AND CO.

C. E. WELDON PRANG AND CO.

Neither Selwyn Image, Charles Ricketts, Lawrence Housman, Heywood Sumner, Louis Davis, nor a dozen other designers, who are peculiarly fitted for the task, have (I believe) one single published example. Here is surely an opportunity for a shrewd manufacturer, if he did but know it.

Not only must many scores of cards by well-known artists, published by the firms already noticed, be left unmentioned here; but firms whose publications embrace hundreds of original designs cannot be discussed, even in the most cursory fashion. Messrs Davidson, whose books are in excellent taste and full of dainty inventions; older firms – Dietrich (who brought out the first monochrome card), Ough, Rothe, Mansell, of Oxford Street (who published charming platinotypes after Frank Miles and others), Meissner & Buch, Schipper, Sockl & Nathan, Phillipe Bros., Ollendorf, Duprez, Geo. Meek, Woods, Yates (of Nottingham), M. H. Nathan & Co., Bollans of Leamington; and those whose speciality was to produce comparatively few cards, with clever sketches, or good ideas, comic and otherwise, in black and white chiefly, such as Albert Gray, Hamilton, Hills & Co., Eugene Rimmel, and last, but by no means least, we have Lowell's (of Boston, U.S.A.) famous series of steel-plate cards.

Then again, the publication of Christmas cards by firms like the Religious Tract Society, T. Nelson & Co., the Society for the Promotion of Christian Knowledge, John Walker & Co., and the Mildmay series must be left out; and the huge number of sham legal documents, old English broadsheets, imitation cheques and bank notes, and the like, cannot be noticed – not even the series of post cards, some imitations, others lithographed on the actual cards, which, from 1871, have appeared from time to time.

It was no doubt inevitable that the thorough working-out of the idea which influenced in slightly different ways the publications of the typical firms I have briefly described, should have exhausted the novelty which the public appears to prize above every other quality. Hence, long before the date when the earliest leaders retired from any effort to maintain the important places they had so honourably won, other

PRANG AND CO.

FRANG.

firms entered with vigour and with a keen sense of the value of judicious advertisement gained by direct and indirect means. Several of these offered large sums of money in prizes, exhibited the designs sent in by competitors at the chief galleries, secured the assistance of artists of high reputation to act as judges, and enlisted the services of many new and already popular artists who had hitherto kept aloof. Yet, with a full recognition of the increased attention paid to reproductions, and the sincere efforts of those concerned to obtain the best designs that money could purchase, one cannot but feel that the simpler cards of early years, with all their crudity of colouring, their comparatively second-rate chromo-lithography, and their occasionally indifferent draughtsmanship in spite of all these very obvious shortcomings, kept a certain direction that was more akin to their purpose than the elaborate compositions of later years. In short, some of these cards were entitled to be ranked among the art-products of the year, whereas the mass of recent cards, with few notable exceptions, are merely bric-à-brac, and of no more intrinsic merit as design or colour, than half the superfluous trifles of the "fancy emporium," the *articles de Paris*, in oxydised metal, rococo, gilt plush, and ormolu, which fill the windows of our best and worst shopping streets, and in debased imitations overflow the baskets on the pavements outside cheap drapery stores. Here is not the place even to enquire how far the sale of cards by the haberdashers, and the consequent cutting of prices affected their art standard. In early years they were chiefly distributed through the booksellers and stationers; now they are in every window—draper, tobacconist, toy shop, and the rest. It would be invidious to attempt to estimate the amount of "culture" possessed by the various traders, but if a man who drives fat oxen should himself be fat—we might argue a man who sells books ought to be more enlightened than one who disposes purely material products. Be that as it may, the introduction of the draper as the middleman first gave an immense impetus to the trade, and then as prices were cut, made it an impossibility for many firms to sustain the battle. It is said that Messrs. Botten and Tidswell, the first drapers who made a feature of Christmas cards, gave in 1880 a single order for £10,000 worth. Compare this item with the turnover of one of the fairly important houses about the same date, which amounted to only £6,000, and one sees that the tendency of this innovation was towards the production of huge editions at low prices, instead of the best class of designs which would attract only an infinitely smaller number of buyers, so that even if they were sold at higher prices there was not anything like the same amount of profit to be made out of them. When people had learned that cards of attractive appearance could be bought at a price per dozen they had hitherto paid for a single one, that the latest patterns of

ALICE B. WOODWARD (PRIVATE)

ALICE B. WOODWARD (PRIVATE)

the season were to be obtained at half-price, or less, at certain places, the question of huge discounts came as the most important factor. In earlier days, cards were purchased leisurely, as people still choose songs, or books, with a great amount of consideration. Afterwards the exigencies of rapid shopping came in, and a "dozen for 4½d." — so many "at 2¼d. each" replaced the cards selected one by one, with a definite recipient in the buyers' minds for each. As the number of cards received and sent grew larger and larger, the personal element disappeared — no longer could the greetings on each card be carefully read, and its sentiments duly weighed, so as to accord with those of its destined receiver. Hence the rapid welcome given to the innocuous private card — a merely formal greeting that was never too warm, or too stilted. But the more the practice became stereotyped to a purely unsentimental convention — a question of etiquette, not amity — so its weakness became apparent, and, year by year, it became more possible to announce that one intended to drop sending Christmas cards, without incurring the reproach of indolence or parsimony by such abstention. The total production, we are told, has never fallen off; even if this statement be accurate — which is extremely uncertain — there is little doubt but that the practice is by no means so universal in "Society" as it was ten years since. Any moment may restore its popularity, but, unless some special influence works to its revival, one would never be surprised to see it become obsolete — even as the custom of sending Valentines has practically died out.

I had hoped to give bibliographies of the work of certain artists of importance, who have been represented by more than a single set of cards, but space entirely forbids it. Yet a few lists, not, I fear, exhaustive in more than a single instance, may be permitted.

Miss Kate Greenaway has preserved no complete set of her own designs — nor have her publishers; hence collectors must needs exercise their ingenuity to discover which of the many unsigned cards that appear to be hers are genuine and which are imitations. After the success of her first popular series (issued, as were the majority, by Marcus Ward), it is easy enough to discard the too-faithful disciples who never once caught her peculiar charm. But in the earlier of hers, when her manner was less pronounced, even the publishers are not always absolutely certain regarding the authorship of several designs. Those indisputably by Miss Greenaway include: a set of children, 1878; another set — a Page in red, with a cup, etc.; children by ponds; a set of little

ALICE B. WOODWARD (PRIVATE)

H. F. NEW (PRIVATE)

people in initial letters; a set of damsels with muffs, and lads in ulsters; another set of four initials; a Red Riding-hood set; an oblong set, with processions of little people; a tiny set of three; an upright set of three single figures; a set of heads; and a set of *Coachmen*, some of which are reproduced here. To these may be added the calendars published by Marcus Ward, as well as the annual "Kate Greenaway's Almanac," published by Geo. Routledge & Sons; a set in circular panels on small cards, published by Goodall; a set, *The Four Seasons*; also a calendar with four designs issued separately as cards, and a few early cards published by Marcus Ward.

Without very minute and tedious detail, it is not possible to identify even those in written descriptions; but, unless collectors have at least as many sets (usually four in each series) as I have noted, they may still be certain that the most prized section of their collection is incomplete. How many more can be traced it would be pleasant to discover. Possibly this publication may lead some generous and fortunate owner of a complete set to divulge further facts regarding it.

That Mr Walter Crane has designed but a few cards, comes as a surprise when one goes into the matter in detail. With fertility of invention, facility of execution, and perfect command of the technique peculiarly suited for colour-printing, it is most curious to discover only two sets – issued in the ordinary way, and one set (printed on a sheet, if memory may be trusted) issued as a supplement for the *Graphic* in (or about) 1875. His first, "The Four Seasons," published by Marcus Ward, & Co., in 1872 or 1873, were small oblong cards in gold and colour, illustrated by groups of children. From the second set, issued some years later, we are allowed to

W. MIDGLEY (PRIVATE)

FRED. MASON (PRIVATE)

PRIVATE CHRISTMAS CARD
BY G. CAVE FRANCE.

A. C. V. LILLY (PRIVATE

reproduce specimens here · therefore description of the designs themselves may be omitted. The couplets on the cards are by the artist himself. The set which appeared in the *Graphic* among various fancies, included "Everybody's Candidate" Father Christmas in his carriage, drawn by people of different classes. A little calendar called "Time's Garland," published by Marcus Ward, was a folding card, with two figures in each of the four panels, and devices on the outer side of the folding "doors" of the card. Another calendar of larger size was also brought out by the same firm. It represented two babies, one attired as the Old Year and the other as the

(PRIVATE)

F. G. JACKSON (PRIVATE)

New, at a party in the Hall. The young one is saying to the old "Must you go so soon?" These, so far as their author is able to remember, and so far as the publishers can trace them, represent the total of Mr Walter Crane's contributions to our subject.

C. M. GERE (PRIVATE)

Mr G. C. Haité, who contributed numerous charming designs for cards and booklets for many publishers, has kindly allowed an example to be illustrated here. It would have been pleasant — but is impracticable — to give a list of the actual sets designed by him which are in circulation, often enough in very inadequate reproductions.

Miss Charlotte Spiers, sister of the architect, whose private cards I have mentioned, designed many sets, all of conspicuous merit. These include the well-known series of open envelope with flowers and a fan-fold "Kakemono" screen, both issued by Marcus Ward; sets of *Red Turk's Cap Lilies*, and of *Iris*, a circular floral set; a set of landscapes with flower swag and a set of landscapes and swallows. Also sets of *Dormice*, *Squirrels*, *Mice*, *Rabbits*, *Kittens*, *Seals*, *White Rats*, *Chickens and Eggs*, *Frogs*, *Donkeys*, *White Mice with banners*, and *Chickens*, all the animals being depicted in admirably decorative convention.

The cards, evidently by Jules Chéret, issued by various firms, deserve tracing, for no artist is more the object of the collector's anxious research at the present time than the Chéret of four hundred *affiches*. Many of these cards are so curiously prophetic of his *Buttes Chaumont* posters, that conscientious collectors should endeavour to bring together a series of his early designs. Here, too, I must notice two monochrome designs by H. S. Marks, R.A., which had escaped the artist's memory when he kindly gave me information of the others. One has a design of a *Poulterer*, another of *Waits*.

SIDNEY HEATH (PRIVATE)

Of the numerous New Year etchings by French artists, many of them most charming productions,

S. THOMPSON (PRIVATE)

it is impossible to speak here. But reference may be made to the delightful design by M. Dillon for M. Octave Uzanne, which is reproduced here by the kind permission of the owner.

In the Christmas card trade, the term "private cards" describes merely those cards which are arranged to bear (whether in ordinary writing or printed by lithography matters not) the name of the sender. These may vary from a simple lettering, with no more a design than is on an ordinary "At Home" card, to a design more or less elaborate, whereof the purchaser orders the required number, and has his own writing added by the publisher, or in other cases a blank space left for the autograph of the sender.

The "private card," as I use the term here, denotes a design made for the individual who despatches it, and strictly limited to his use. As a rule it is the handiwork of the sender; therefore, it is not surprising that, so far, the custom is almost entirely confined to artists.

WALTER LANGLEY, R.I. (PRIVATE)

WALTER LANGLEY, R.I. (PRIVATE)

But what the artist does to-day, Society has a knack of doing to-morrow, and already signs of the new departure are not wanting.

Another distinguishing mark of these cards is their almost invariable employment of monochrome, which is easily explained by the prohibitive cost of chromo-lithography when concerned with small numbers. Of course very many cards sent out each year from the so-called "hand-painted" of the better class of shops, to the genuine sketch in water-colour or oils by artists of repute, must also be included technically as Christmas cards, if they bear an inscription which adapts them for the purpose. But such unique instances, whether good or bad, are not within the actual limits of our subject. It is obvious that any sketch or design may be, by arbitrary lettering, turned to a genuine Christmas card; yet every etching, print, or photograph can also be as readily perverted to this use, so that the number might be widened indefinitely. For if any print or drawing, plus a Christmas motto added by the sender, comes within the boundary, why not any booklet, or any book? To consider then, an encyclopædia in fifty quarto volumes, turned to a veritable

FROM AN ETCHING BY
R. W. MACBETH, A.R.A.

ALFRED EAST, R.I. (PRIVATE)

"Christmas card" by inscribing "With Christmas Wishes" on the fly-leaf of Volume One, would be merely the carrying of such an argument to its logical, but ridiculous, conclusion.

Therefore, the designs illustrated or noticed here are confined to those made for the purpose, reproduced in sufficient numbers by etching, lithography, woodcut, or "process," and deliberately planned with the object of conveying a greeting. This does not imply that each must needs show a seasonable or appropriate design, nor even that the lettering may not be a mere addition to the drawing, and without relation to the design, or an integral part of the scheme of decoration employed.

Among the earliest examples of these private cards, some by J. Goddard, of Leicester, must be placed first, not merely for their date, 1870, but because they were lithographed in as many as six colours, including gold and silver, and in all respects typical and admirable examples of the ideal card; a series by Walter Spiers, including at least seven varieties, and others by E. H. Birch. That these gentlemen all chance to be architects is collateral evidence of the theory I advanced before knowing of the existence of these cards.

Naturally, etchers have been among the first to send their friends specimens of their own work as a Christmas greeting because an etcher can (and as a rule does) print as many of his own plates as he requires for personal use. So R. W. Macbeth, Wilfrid Ball, Axel H. Haig, Charles J. Watson, Edward Slocombe, Alfred East, W. J. Wainwright, Walter Langley, W. L. Wyllie, Herbert Dicksee, and other etchers, figure amongthose reproduced. Next to them come those who cut their own wood blocks, or work in intimate relation with fellow artists who are engravers—these include: C. M. Gere, E. H. New, and Sidney Heath. Next in order are those accustomed to draw for publication—Alice B. Woodward, Stanley Thompson, and Frank G. Jackson. Thus the examples reproduced so fully bear out the theory put forward above that in no single instance is it controverted.

Yet, instances where the theory could not hold good are to be found—also cases where a

WILFRID BALL, R.P.E. (PRIVATE)

E. SLOCOMBE, R.P.E. (PRIVATE)

W. J. WAINWRIGHT, A.R.W.S. (PRIVATE)

special design has been commissioned to be used by the laity. It is this fashion which (speaking on the side of the designer) seems worthy of more notice than has hitherto been accorded to it. Possibly, young artists might find it worth their while to prepare specimens, and put them on view in certain fashionable shops, some time in October—or earlier—so that clients could prepare their own cards in due time for the colonial mails. If the fashion spread as quickly as others have done in recent years, the book plate craze for instance, it might prove a welcome industry for the trained art student who has need

C. J. WATSON, R.P.E. (PRIVATE)

of any and every source of income in the period when his school work is over, but editors are still blind to his talent, as he hawks a portfolio from door to door in vain.

It has, perhaps, too often been held beneath the dignity of artists to look ahead and provide craftsmen with designs capable of direct paraphrase. Surely it is better art to master the facts and control them beforehand, than to leave a mechanic to revise the designs to adapt them for practicable working. For a stained window, it is good that the designer

FROM AN ETCHING BY
EDWARD SLOCOMBE, R.P.E.

W. L. WYLLIE, A.R.A. (PRIVATE)

should think not only of the necessary leads, but for the equally essential ties of iron which cross the panel vertically; if for a marble statue, it were folly for the sculptor to scheme details that might be the easiest problem for a metal-worker to carry out but absolutely impossible in stone. We grant this in many of the arts; why, therefore, should we not ask of the illustrator that he masters the after-technique which reproduces his work, so far as he can control it, by choosing the most direct mechanism to express his ideas? It is splendidly independent, no doubt, to say that "the artist is not concerned with mechanics it is their business to carry out his ideas;" but if they cannot do so, without ruining the whole, owing to the needlessly unsuitable scheme he has chosen, would his work be less fettered in the end, if he kept it from the first within the limits where the very best result comes naturally and easily?

HERBERT DICKSEE, R.P.E. (PRIVATE)

One word of personal explanation may be permitted me before closing a hasty survey of a big subject big, that is, so far as mere numbers are concerned. The illustrations selected by the Editor of *The Studio* have been chosen not necessarily for their artistic merit alone, but as a representative series of typical examples of the best designs in many different styles; and it is pleasant to record the unanimous consent of all concerned, by whose permission so many notable designs are illustrated. The opinions put forward and the facts quoted are set down without any commercial bias, with no partisan feeling, and without prejudice. In so rapid a sketch, reiteration is almost inevitable, and omission, I fear, no less unlikely. Special thanks

WILFRID BALL, R.P.E. (PRIVATE)

RANDOLPH CALDECOTT (PRIVATE)

to Mr Jonathan King, *the* collector *par excellence;* to Mr C. W. Faulkner, Mr Thomas Crane (Marcus Ward & Co.), Mr Ackermann (Prang's), Mr R. E. Mack (Ernest Nister), Mr Harris (S. Hildesheimer & Co.), Mr. McCabe (C. Goodall & Sons), Messrs De la Rue & Co., Mr Adolphe Tuck, and to Mr R. Phené Spiers, Mr H. S. Marks, R.A., Mr W. C. T. Dobson, R.A., and Mr J. E. Horsley, R.A., for varying degrees of help not adequately acknowledged by this brief recognition are due, from theirs, very faithfully,

GLEESON WHITE.

[The thanks of the Editor are specially due to Mr F. G. Jackson, Mr Wilfrid Ball, Mr F. Goulding and Mr W. H. Ward for assistance in the selection of suitable cards, and to the Swan Electric Engraving Co., and to Messrs André & Sleigh for the excellent manner in which they have reproduced them.]

DILLON [DESIGNED FOR A PRIVATE CARD FOR M. OCTAVE UZANNE]

www.ingramcontent.com/pod-product-compliance
Lightning Source LLC
Chambersburg PA
CBHW020239030726
47497CB00009B/3173
9783337262624